ABOUT WOMEN

D.B. WRIGHT

99 Hearts Publishing

San Francisco, CA

D.B. Wright / 99 Hearts Publishing
www.99heartspub.com

Publisher's Note: This is a work of fiction. Names, characters, places, and incidents are a product of the author's imagination. Locales and public names are sometimes used for atmospheric purposes. Any resemblance to actual people, living or dead, or to businesses, companies, events, institutions, or locales is completely coincidental.

A special thanks to Darryl & Robin Wright -who are in fact very real and not a product of the author's imagination.

Author Illustration by George Bordeanu
http://georgebordeanu.blogspot.ro

About Women / D.B. Wright -- 1st ed.
ISBN 978-0-6924874-1-9

For all the women, everywhere

"What would men be without women? Scarce, sir...mighty scarce."

—MARK TWAIN

CONTENTS

CHAPTER ONE

ABOUT WOMEN

I have a great urge to write,
and to write about women

but I know nothing about them,

so I am silent.

Nevertheless –being of sound mind and stout heart and after a decade and a half of research I will now share what I have come to know for sure about them..

Everything I know about women.

I DO LOVE THEM, THOUGH

I do love them, though.

.

THE END.

AFTERWORD

Finally,
If you have taken this too seriously,
you might've missed the point entirely.

If you don't know what to do,
take this book, use it as a journal.
Fill it with what *you* know,
or what you learn,
about women.

Then share it.

It can only help everyone.

#aboutwomen

ABOUT THE AUTHOR

D.B. Wright is a writer, poet, and satirist of our generation.
This is his first serious attempt at the novel.